Brevkort.

(Paa denne Side skrives kun Adressen.)

Til

For Ina — a cherished sister, a great aunt. — KM

For Antoinette who, at ninety-five,
still drives her own car. — BR

SER. 127

A merry Christmas!

The author extends his
sincere thanks to Nora for
her faith in the story.

Groundwood Books / House of Anansi Press
110 Spadina Avenue, Suite 801, Toronto, Ontario M5V 2K4
Distributed in the USA by Publishers Group West
1700 Fourth Street, Berkeley, CA 94710

We acknowledge for their financial support of our publishing program the
Canada Council for the Arts, the Government of Canada through the Book
Publishing Industry Development Program (BPIDP) and the Ontario Arts Council.

ONTARIO ARTS COUNCIL
CONSEIL DES ARTS DE L'ONTARIO

Nr. 298

Library and Archives Canada Cataloguing in Publication
Major, Kevin
Aunt Olga's Christmas postcards / Kevin Major ; illustrations by Bruce Roberts.
ISBN 0-88899-593-8
1. Christmas stories, Canadian (English) I. Roberts, Bruce
II. Title.
PS8576.A523A96 2005   jC813'.54   C2005-901275-7

The illustrations are in India and colored inks and watercolor
on high-gloss Japanese paper

Book design by Michael Solomon   Printed and bound in China

AUNT OLGA'S CHRISTMAS POSTCARDS

✶✶✶✶✶✶✶✶✶✶✶✶

KEVIN MAJOR

ILLUSTRATIONS BY

BRUCE ROBERTS

A GROUNDWOOD BOOK

HOUSE OF ANANSI PRESS

TORONTO BERKELEY

Joyeux Noël

Great-great *Aunt Olga* is ninety-five. She calls herself a nonagenarian! We all think the world of her.

"She's amazing," my mother says.

"She's quite the gal, all right," my father says. "Even if she isn't as sharp as she used to be."

"I buy her purple and she refuses to wear it."

"Suddenly all she will wear is red," adds my father, shaking his head.

She's just being Aunt Olga, that's all. She loves red! It's because Christmas is her favorite time of the year.

Aunt Olga writes poetry and does tai chi and reads travel magazines. She collects Christmas postcards from around the world. My father says that some of them are as old as she is and just as rare.

FRÖHLICHE WEIHNACHTEN

Aunt Olga calls to ask if I can come over to her house on the Saturday before Christmas Day.

"You don't have to go if you don't want to, Anna," my mother whispers. "Things are just not the same."

But I have to see Aunt Olga. Christmas is our special time together.

"I'll be there, Aunt Olga," I tell her.

HELLO, FOLKS!
A MERRY CHRISTMAS TO YOU ALL

A Merry Christmas

I arrive after lunch on Saturday. I can smell gingerbread as soon as my father turns into the driveway.

"Be patient, angel," he says as I wave good-bye.

I run as fast as I can through the snow to the front door.

"Merry Christmas… Veselé Vánoce. God Jul. Frohe Weihnachten," Aunt Olga calls from the kitchen.

Aunt Olga can speak a lot of different languages.

"Joyeux Noël!" I sing out. I can speak only two.

I hang up my coat and put my winter boots neatly by the door.

Aunt Olga is sitting in her favorite place at the kitchen table. I hug and kiss her.

The smell of gingerbread is more wonderful than ever.

"We'll mix the icing so we can decorate the cookies. Want to?" I ask.

Aunt Olga runs her fingers through her thin, silver hair.

"This year we'll leave the cookies plain. They're just as tasty."

Aunt Olga smiles. She is remembering something, I think. I see a tear in her eye.

"Will you get the box, Anna?" she asks, and her smile takes
the tear away.

I know right where the box is kept.

I walk back slowly, one step at a time, and place it gently
on the table.

Aunt Olga brushes her hand over the wood.

"My brother, Stefan, loved Christmas. And he loved to
carve wood. Before he went away he made this box, and under
the tree that Christmas it was left for me. Inside was my very
first Christmas postcard."

Aunt Olga tells me that story every Christmas. But this
year, for the very first time, she takes out the postcard for me
to see.

"One Christmas," Aunt Olga says, "I wrote a poem for Stefan."

Candles light the battlefield snow
A brother remembers a Christmas
when soldiers were tin
and guns were tree limbs
And all the world glowed.

"I tried to write more lines," says Aunt Olga, "but I never could."

"It's wonderful just as it is," I tell her.

I have questions to ask Aunt Olga about her brother.

"The gingerbread," she says, before I have a chance. "We mustn't forget the gingerbread."

I help Aunt Olga open the oven door. She takes out the gingerbread cookies and puts them on the kitchen counter. I help her back to her chair.

When the cookies are cool I bite into one. They're still the best.

"Aren't you going to have a cookie, Aunt Olga?"

"I really don't need the calories," Aunt Olga says, "if I'm ever going to dance again."

She is still thinking about long, long ago.

Wishing you a Merry Xmas. and a Happy New Year.

"Show me the postcards, Aunt Olga."

She looks through her box. "Here I am. In my prime!"

"You were gorgeous. Absolutely gorgeous!"

Aunt Olga laughs. "Wasn't I something else? What a stunning outfit, don't you think? Wasn't I slim?"

We always have such fun, pretending.

"Didn't you write a poem about it, Aunt Olga?"

"I did. Yes, I did."

MAY·YOUR·CHRISTMAS
BE·A·VERY·HAPPY·ONE·AND
YOUR·NEW·YEAR·BRIGHT
·AND·PROSPEROUS·

A Merry Christmas

CHRISTMAS WISHES·

CHRISTMAS BELLS

As the bells ring on
Christmas Day
My thoughts go ringing
out your way
To wish this day your
life may bless
And fill your heart
with happiness.

To extend
CHRISTMAS GREETINGS
and to wish you
NEW YEAR HAPPINESS.

A Merry Christmas
Many happy years, unbroken
Friendships, and cheerful recollections.

I was the belle of the Christmas ball.
I was the flower against the wall.
I took a boy's hand
I took it, then twirled
and out on the floor I whirled and
    whirled
until he was dizzy and fell in a heap
and I soared over him in a flying leap!
Oh, I was the belle of the Christmas
    ball...
he just wilted against the wall.

We laugh and laugh.

It takes her a long time, but Aunt Olga makes tea. Never before did she think I should have tea and never before in her special Christmas china.

"How did you ever get to be so funny, Aunt Olga? Tell me again."

"The first job I ever had was writing verses for Christmas postcards," Aunt Olga says. There is new excitement in her words. "There weren't cards to put in envelopes, like there are now. Just postcards. Not every postcard needed a verse, but if it did, it was my job to write it."

Aunt Olga sips her tea and laughs.

MERRY CHRISTMAS

May Santa fill your Christmas tree
With gifts of health and cheer;
And nothing mar your happiness,
Throughout the coming year.

W549

"Heavens, I wrote some wretched stuff! I tried to be funny, but they didn't want anything funny. They wanted boring old sugary verse."

"What did you do?"

"I had no choice. I needed the money. But in the evenings I went home and wrote what I really wanted to write."

"Are they all about Christmas?"

Aunt Olga nods. "And Christmas postcards are my inspiration, Anna."

HEUREUX NOËL

Noël! un doux rayon vermeil,
De ton radieux nom, se dégage;
Réconfortant tous les coeurs,
Et leur apportant du bonheur.

CHRISTMAS GREETINGS.

I wrote Santa your address and
Told him The way,
So he surely will find you on
Christmas Day.

"Look at these," Aunt Olga says, with even more excitement in her voice. She searches through the box. "These were made from real pictures."

She spreads them out on the table.

"Here I am! That's me when I was your age, bringing home a Christmas tree. See the touch of red on my coat!"

"I do, Aunt Olga."

"Well, maybe it's not me..."

"You can't have doubts, Aunt Olga. You have to believe, really believe. It's no fun if you don't."

"Of course... Imagine having to wear angel wings to get your picture taken!"

"Itchy," I say. "You must have hated it."

"I did. I did."

Aunt Olga turns over several postcards before she finds the right one. "Here it is," she says. "I wrote it on the back of this card. My very first angel poem."

❄❄❄❄❄❄❄

*Being an angel is not always
  easy
especially on a day when it's
  suddenly breezy
for if caught in a gale
you are sure to fishtail
and take a nosedive
that you might not survive.
Heavens! It's unsafe and far,
  far too wild
being a darling, adorable,
  angelic child!*

Sainte Cécile

Fauvette
1439

Rõõmsaid Jõulu pühi

Gesegnete
Weihnachten

EAS
4761/4

"Oh, Aunt Olga!"

"I was mad about rhyme in those days," Aunt Olga says, shaking her head. "Absolutely mad."

"Did your father call you his angel, too?" I ask, still laughing.

Aunt Olga nods.

She looks at me and quickly adds, "But angels can have a great time, can't they, Anna?"

"Of course, a great, great time!"

"I had a scooter, just like you do. And a sled. But skating was my favorite. I loved to dance on ice."

"I do, too. When we're on ice we almost fly. We're really angels, then."

Gelukkig Nieuwjaar

When autumn days slip into winter
and the ponds run thick with ice
it is then my spirit races
and my heart soars in flight.
I am a gentle, earthbound sister
Winter lifts me to boundless heights.

"Because we're angels, we think like angels," I tell Aunt Olga. "At Christmas we must remember the happiest things."

Aunt Olga nods slowly. "Sometimes it is harder when you are old."

"You're not old, really, Aunt Olga. Pretend, just pretend. We're the best at that."

She smiles.

"You start," I say. "Think of one good thing that angels bring."

Now there is a sparkle in Aunt Olga's eyes. "I think you have the makings of a poet, Anna."

Aunt Olga searches out some more of her angel postcards.

> *One good thing that angels bring*
> *is the Child of God, the King of Kings*

"Now it's your turn," Aunt Olga says to me.
"Really?"
"Think hard. Something good is bound to come."
I look at the postcards for inspiration.

> *One good thing that angels bring…*
> *is a Christmas bell to ring and ring*

"Good! My turn."

Another fine thing that angels bring
Are Christmas carols for all to sing

I am thinking hard again.

Another fine thing that angels
bring
Is a tall fir tree with lights to
string

"Of course poems shouldn't have to rhyme," says Aunt Olga.

An angel comes striding into
town
baskets brimming with delights
Make way, make way!

"Is that really a poem, Aunt Olga?"
"It could be, with some work. Now your turn."
"Oh, no."

It's Christmas Eve
Old Father Christmas has lost
his way
The toys are getting restless
Make way! Make way!
Angel to the rescue.

Loving Christmas
Wishes from

Blow your horn, angel boy
Clear the path
Slide on down
the slippery slope
to heaven.

I'm the angel queen of
*   Christmas*
royally sitting in my sleigh
Santa does all the pushing
I sit back and...and...
Smile!

"Oh, heavens!" says Aunt Olga.

All our fun gives Aunt Olga an idea.

"We'll each write a poem. We'll make it our Christmas present to each other!"

"But I'm not a poet. Not like you, Aunt Olga."

"Everyone has poetry inside them. It just needs a reason to come out."

Aunt Olga is so cheery that I know I can't let her down.

"But what will I write about?"

"It must be something you feel in your heart," Aunt Olga whispers. "That's all."

I try as hard as I can, but my mind is still blank.

Aunt Olga pushes the postcard box in front of me. "A little inspiration?"

When your Christmas world is full of woe
Don't sit and groan under mistletoe
Check out Santa, then you'll know
To let loose a smile and let it grow
Chuckle and giggle high and low
Explode in laughter head to toe
Ho ho ho ho ho ho HO!

Herzlichen
Glückwunsch
zum neuen Jahre

A MERRY
CHRISTMAS

I hope you will
get all you
expect

A JOLLY GOOD CHRISTMAS.

"What do you think?" I ask Aunt Olga.

She looks at me and frowns.

"I couldn't help it, Aunt Olga. I'm mad about rhyme. Absolutely mad."

Her frown changes to a smile. Her smile changes to a laugh. "It flies off the page! It must be the work of an angel!"

Being a poet is awesome. Aunt Olga needs lots of changes to get her poem right. I help her out all I can.

By the time she is finished it is getting dark outside. We light candles, then sit next to each other sipping tea and munching on gingerbread cookies.

Now Aunt Olga is ready to read her poem out loud.

"Here I go," she says. "Can I still fly… I wonder?"

The Christmas day is icy cold
the air is filled with winter fun
Out on the lake skaters gather
Hand in hand.

Herzlichen Glückwunsch
zum neuen Jahre

I think I want again to glide
to stride and swirl without a care
to let the fresh air catch my face
before today slips into night.

If my heart serves me true
and all my memories remain
then I will dance another day
and in his eyes
find peace... again.

Now there is a tear in my eye.
"Oh, Aunt Olga."
We hug each other.

A MERRY CHRISTMAS

DESIGN COPYRIGHTED, JOHN WINSCH, 1912

We both look at the clock on the kitchen wall. My father will soon be coming to pick me up.

Aunt Olga stands up slowly and brings a red hat from the hall closet.

She puts it on my head. "Now you are an official Christmas poet!"

"Aunt Olga, you are so much fun."

"Pretty good for a nonagenarian." She laughs.

❊

I put on my winter coat and boots.

Aunt Olga slowly gathers the postcards into the box and closes the lid.

Then she places the box gently in my hands. "I want you to have them, Anna."

"But, Aunt Olga, you can't give away your postcards."

"I'll remember them, Anna. I know I will. And you'll bring them when you come to visit. You have all those Christmases ahead of you, Anna. You'll be needing to write a few poems."

❊❊❊❊❊❊

Aunt Olga lies down on her living-room sofa. Her face shines in the glow of the white lights from the little tree she puts up every Christmas.

"Right now, it's my nap time," Aunt Olga says.

Outside my father is tapping the horn of our car.

I cover Aunt Olga with a blanket, a cozy red one, and kiss her on the cheek.

I blow out the candles on the kitchen table. As soon as I get home I am going to write a poem about Aunt Olga.

"Merry Christmas, angel," Aunt Olga calls out as she falls away to sleep. "Veselé Vánoce. God Jul. Frohe Weihnachten."

"Joyeux Noël, angel," I call back quietly, before closing Aunt Olga's front door and dancing away over the snow.

A NOTE ON CHRISTMAS POSTCARDS

THE FINEST CHRISTMAS POSTCARDS appeared a century ago. Outstanding artists and expensive inks produced these miniature works of art. They might have been "real photos" set up in a studio, wonderfully detailed sketches or fancy, rich embossings. The image of Santa Claus—in his many costumes, from Père Noël to Saint Nicholas—was a particular favorite. Christmas postcards give us a glimpse into history and into Christmas celebrations around the world. Many people find those sent from the soldiers and nurses of World War One especially touching.

The Christmas postcard gave way to the folded card sent inside an envelope. But handmade postcards can still bring Christmas cheer to a relative or friend. Cut a rectangle of sturdy card stock to the size of a regular postcard. Decorate the front in your own special way. Divide the back in half to make space for your message, the address and a lovely Christmas stamp. Drop it into a mailbox, and off into the world goes a Christmas treat. Perhaps a century from now your postcard will find its way into the hands of a collector of postcards in some distant land, someone who will take great delight in a keepsake of a Yuletide long ago.

KM

Buon Natale

A MERRY CHRISTMAS

GOD JUL

tillönskas av broder john

A Merry Christmas to you.

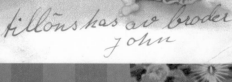
Vom Himmel durch die tiefsten Klüfte Ein milder
Stern hernieder lacht Vom Tannenwalde steigen
Düfte Und helle wird die Winternacht

Herzliche Weihnachtsgrüße